JUST GRANDMA AND

BY MERCER MAYER

A GOLDEN BOOK • NEW YORK
Western Publishing Company, Inc., Racine, Wisconsin 53404

We went to the beach,
just Grandma and me.

I wanted to set up the beach umbrella,

but the wind was too strong.

I bought hot dogs for Grandma and me,
but they fell in the sand.
So I washed them off.

I found a nice seashell for Grandma,
but it was full of a crab.

I wanted to blow up my sea horse,
but I didn't have enough air.
So Grandma helped a little.

I told Grandma to take me
way out in the deep water,

but not too far.

I put on my fins and my mask
and showed Grandma how I can snorkel.

I dug a hole in the sand for Grandma.
Then I covered her up and tickled her toes.

I built a sandcastle just for Grandma, but a big wave came.

Grandma said that's what happens
to sandcastles, and we will build
a new one next time.

On the way home Grandma was tired,
so I told her I would watch for our stop.

We had a good time at the beach,
just Grandma and me.